THE
EAGLE
HAS LANDED

by Jenny Jinks and Gustavo Mazali

W
FRANKLIN WATTS
LONDON•SYDNEY

THE EAGLE HAS LANDED

CONTENTS

Chapter 1	July 16 – Take-off	4
Chapter 2	July 19 – The Moon	11
Chapter 3	July 20 – A Rocky Landing	15
Chapter 4	July 20 – A Giant Leap	20
Chapter 5	July 21 – Footprints on the Moon	24
Chapter 6	July 22 – Going Home	26

CHAPTER 1
JULY 16 - TAKE-OFF

Apollo 11 Transmission

LAUNCH CONTROL: *This is Apollo Saturn Launch Control. We've passed the six-minute mark on our countdown for Apollo 11, the flight to land the first men on the Moon. We are on time. Good luck and Godspeed.*

ARMSTRONG: *Thank you very much. We know it's going to be a good flight.*

LAUNCH CONTROL: *Four minutes and counting. We are go for Apollo 11 – T-minus sixty seconds and counting.*

ARMSTRONG: *It's been a real smooth countdown.*

LAUNCH CONTROL: *... 10 ... 9 ... Ignition sequence started ... 6 ... 5 ... 4 ... 3 ... 2 ...1 ... 0 ... All engines running. Lift-off. We have a lift-off.*

Ever since Neil Armstrong's father had first taken him up in a plane when he was six years old, he had known that he wanted to fly. But being commander of the first manned mission to the Moon was beyond even his wildest dreams. He could hardly believe it even now, as he sat squashed in the tiny command module of the *Saturn V* with his fellow astronauts. Lunar Module Pilot Edwin "Buzz" Aldrin and Command Module Pilot Michael Collins were busy preparing for launch.

The whole world was watching, waiting to see the historic moment when man would land on the Moon. Neil just hoped everything went to plan. Tension began to build as the importance of what they were about to do sank in.

"Ready?" Buzz turned to the others as the countdown ticked down.

"Ready as I'll ever be," Neil replied, his sombre face not giving away how nervous he was feeling.

Suddenly a deep, deafening rumble filled the cabin. *Saturn V* began to rattle and shake as the thrusters fired up underneath them. The main engines had ignited.

"This is it," Michael said, and each of the astronauts drew a deep breath as smoke and flames began to pour out of the rocket below them. Finally, the rocket gave a massive kick, shaking and juddering as it accelerated upwards, off the launch pad, away from Earth, and up towards the stars. They had lift-off!

The rocket was travelling at 100 miles an hour before it had even cleared the launch tower. The thrust forced the astronauts down, pinning them back into their chairs until they couldn't move a muscle. An ear-splitting screech outside sent a shiver down Neil's spine as the rocket fought its way skywards, ripping through the Earth's atmosphere. The rocket continued to rise higher and higher, faster and faster.

Then, just as suddenly as it had started, the screeching

ended. The vibration eased off. Everything went eerily

silent. Neil looked around. The sudden change

in pressure made it feel like everything had stopped.

Then a pen floated slowly up past his face. They were

in zero gravity. They had made it into orbit. He glanced

at the clock. Had it really only been just over ten minutes

since take-off? It had felt like a lifetime already.

The shuttle turned and the breathtaking sight of the Earth,

gleaming far below them, came into view.

"Isn't it beautiful?" Buzz said. "Quick, pass me the camera."

Michael sent the camera spinning, as if in slow motion,

towards him. Buzz tried to catch it, but it floated past him

and hit the window. It would take a while for

the astronauts to get used to zero gravity, even though

they had experienced it before.

Neil took off his helmet and gloves and watched, fascinated, as they floated away from him. He drifted towards the window and stared out at the endless blanket of space that stretched before them. This was just the beginning, he knew. Soon it would be time for the hard work to start.

Saturn V orbited the Earth while the astronauts waited patiently for news from mission control. Then finally, they got the go-ahead they had been waiting for:

HOUSTON: *Apollo 11, this is Houston. Radio check. Over.*
ALDRIN: *Roger, Houston. Apollo 11 loud and clear.*
HOUSTON: *You are go for translunar injection. Over.*
COLLINS: *Apollo 11. Thank you.*

Neil turned to his crewmates. "This is it, guys. Looks like it's time to head to the Moon."

CHAPTER 2
JULY 19 - THE MOON

"There it is, in all its splendour," Michael said, peering out

of his small window as the Moon came into view again,

each time a little closer and clearer than the last.

"It's amazing how it doesn't feel weird at all now

to look out there and see the Moon."

"It's certainly worth the trip," Neil said.

"Well, you'd better get used to it, because we're going

to be seeing a lot more of it," Buzz laughed, taking

a few more pictures on his camera. He wanted to record

every single moment.

"I thought it would be more colourful," Michael said. They had been travelling for three days, and they were finally approaching lunar orbit. The closer they got to the Moon, the more detail they could see. It looked like a vast expanse of solid grey, as if it was made from metal, and covered in deep craters and tall mountains.

It was almost unbelievable to think that in a few minutes they would be landing down there for the very first time. It was nearly time for Buzz and Neil to climb into the lunar module, which would separate from the space shuttle and descend to the Moon. Everyone was beginning to feel nervous.

"Look at that crater," Neil said, pointing to

the lunar surface. "That's some rough terrain down there."

"Look at the mountains. They're huge." Michael said.

"You could spend a lifetime studying just that one crater."

"Must have been one huge meteor to have made

that dent," Buzz added.

"I sure hope none of those meteors come by right now,"

Michael muttered to himself, as he peered out at

the vast emptiness of space. The three men fell silent

as they realised just how vulnerable they were, floating

around in space. That night, as they settled down

to get some rest, the importance of what they were

about to do weighed heavily on their minds.

The following morning, Neil and Buzz began

their preparations to move into the lunar module,

nicknamed *Eagle*, that would take them down

to the surface of the Moon.

"Make sure you guys come back, okay?" Michael told

them, as Buzz and Neil climbed through the connecting

hatch into the tiny module. Michael was to stay inside

the command module, *Columbia*, orbiting the Moon and

waiting for their safe return. Neil took one last look

back, nodded, and then sealed the door.

Michael watched the small landing module drift away.

He hoped, more than anything, that this would not be

the last time he saw his friends.

CHAPTER 3
JULY 20 – A ROCKY LANDING

The journey down to the surface began smoothly.
Eagle was flying on auto-pilot, taking them directly to a
pre-planned landing site in a flat area known as
the Sea of Tranquility. But not long into the descent,
an alarm began to sound. Something was wrong.
"What's going on?" said Neil frantically, as he scanned
the instrument panel in front of him.

"I don't know," Buzz said, flicking switches and trying
to work out what the problem was. But nothing he did
seemed to fix it.

They radioed down to mission control, but the team there couldn't work out what was wrong. What if the *Eagle* was not able to land? Or worse, what if they ended up stranded on the Moon?

"Do we abort?" Buzz hovered his finger over the button that would fire them back up to lunar orbit. If he pressed it, there would be no turning back. Their chance to land on the Moon would be gone.

"No, wait!" Neil said. "If the engine cuts out we'll just drift down to the Moon anyway. Let's stick to the mission." They were so close. He couldn't give up yet.

With alarms sounding, the men tried to stay focused as the lunar module came down to land. But as they got nearer to the planned landing site, they came across another very big problem.

"Look at all those craters!" Buzz said. "They told us it was flat!"

The landing site looked like a boulder field. It would be almost impossible to land safely on such uneven ground. "Some of those rocks are as big as cars," Buzz said. "What are we going to do?" Then, as suddenly as it started, the alarm stopped.

"Right," said Neil decidedly. "We have to find a different site." Buzz nodded in agreement. Neil switched off the auto-pilot and took control of *Eagle*, steering it away from the landing site. He hoped he would be able to find a more suitable spot in time. Every slight change in direction was using up more and more precious fuel. Then the alarm began to sound again.

"What now?" Neil asked, trying to stay calm.

"I don't know. Just focus on landing this thing," Buzz said, flicking more switches to try to shut the alarm off. Neil watched tensely as they approached a crater. "How's the fuel?" he asked Buzz.

"We're down to eight per cent. We need to land *now*," Buzz replied.

Neil began to steer them across the huge hole.

"Wait," he said suddenly, "I think I can see something."

He was sure he could make out a clear, flat area just the other side of a ridge. This was their last chance. Another minute and they would have to abort the mission. Gently, he began to lower the *Eagle* down. "Nearly there," he murmured, holding his breath as they slowly lowered closer to the surface of the Moon.

"Okay, we are coming down nicely," Buzz said, keeping a close eye on the control panel. "Picking up some dust." The *Eagle* moved down slowly, just clearing the edge of the crater as Neil engaged the landing gear.

"Contact light," Buzz said. "We're down."

With a slight bump, *Eagle* settled on the Moon.

ARMSTRONG: *Houston – Tranquility Base here.*

THE EAGLE HAS LANDED.

HOUSTON: *Roger, Tranquility, we copy you on*

the ground. You got a bunch of guys about to turn blue.

We're breathing again. Thanks a lot.

Cheers rose up around mission control in Houston.
They had made it – the first manned lunar module
had landed successfully. Man was on the Moon!

CHAPTER 4
JULY 20 - A GIANT LEAP

Neil took a deep, steadying breath, and opened the hatch.
200,000 miles below them, back on Earth, more than
half a billion people tuned in their TVs and radios,
waiting eagerly for the historic moment when humankind
would first set foot on the Moon. Carefully, Neil squeezed
out of the hatch and began to climb down the ladder.
The last step was a lot further down than intended, and he
had to jump to reach the surface. But, at long last, he was
there. He was the first man ever to set foot on the Moon.
"That's one small step for man ... one giant leap for
mankind," he said, the words catching in his throat.

"What's it like?" Michael asked, from high above them in *Columbia*. How he wished he could be down there experiencing it for himself. Neil looked around at the vast, empty landscape of this strange new world he found himself on. "The surface looks grey with a very fine covering, almost like a powder," he reported. "It's like the desert. It's beautiful."

Buzz gazed around, awestruck at the sight before him. It was strange and alien. The land under their feet seemed to glow, almost too sharp and clear to be believed. The sky above was like a huge black void, empty and starless. The only other thing visible was the Earth, hanging in the sky thousands of miles away.

They took a few hesitant first steps, trying to find their feet. It was a strange sensation, walking with scarcely any gravity to hold them down, and it took a while to gain control over their movements. They were slow and clumsy, and the surface was surprisingly slippery.

21

"It takes two or three paces to make sure you've got your feet underneath you," Buzz laughed as he slipped on the fine soil, lost control, and landed flat on his face.

But there wasn't much time for fun and games. They had a full schedule of reports and experiments to carry out, and only a short time to get everything done.

They collected samples of dust and rock in various sizes, shapes and textures, all ready to take home and be studied.

They set up science experiments, reported on conditions, and, of course, took countless photos.

"I could stay up here for days," Buzz said, staring around at the unbelievable view.

But unfortunately they were already running out of time. There was just time for a very special phone call from President Nixon, the President of the United States.

NIXON: *Hello, Neil and Buzz. This certainly has to be the most historic phone call ever made from the Oval Office. I just can't tell you how proud we all are of what you've done ...*

ARMSTRONG: *Thank you, Mr President. It's a great honour and privilege for us to be here.*

CHAPTER 5

JULY 21 - FOOTPRINTS ON THE MOON

After just two and a half hours, it was time to head back. The two astronauts collected their samples and took everything back to the *Eagle*. Before they left, they placed a small silicon plaque on the Moon with messages from world leaders. As Neil climbed back up the ladder, he glanced down at the plaque. It read: "Here men from the planet Earth first set foot upon the Moon July 1969, A. D. We came in peace for all mankind."

"I did it," Neil whispered to himself. "I really did it." As they sealed the hatch behind them, they looked down and saw their footprints left behind in the moon dust. It was nice to know that part of them would always be up there. They had made their mark on history. And now it was time to go home.

24

A few hours later, exhausted and bleary-eyed, it was time to leave the Moon behind. But something was wrong.

"The engine won't start," Neil said, puzzled.

Buzz went to check the circuit board. There was a hole where the switch should be. "The switch is broken off," he said, panic clear in his voice. "We can't take off without it. We'll be stuck here!"

The pair searched frantically around the module for anything that might fix the problem, but for all the backup plans and spare parts they had, there was nothing that could fit the small gap and close the circuit.

Then Buzz had a flash of inspiration. He reached into the top shoulder pocket of his suit and pulled out a pen. He jammed the end of it into the hole where the switch belonged. It worked! The circuit breaker held in place, and the engine roared into life.

"Looks like we'll be going home after all," Buzz laughed.

CHAPTER 6
JULY 22 - GOING HOME

LOVELL: Eagle and Columbia, *this is the backup crew.* Our congratulations for yesterday's performance, and our prayers are with you for the rendezvous. Over.

ARMSTRONG: Thank you, Jim.

COLLINS: Thank you, Jim.

ARMSTRONG: *Glad to have all you beautiful people looking over our shoulders. We had a lot of help down there, Jim.*

When *Eagle* had finally returned to *Columbia*, Collins had breathed a sigh of relief. It had been a lonely time without the others. They had had so many things stacked against them. But now, for the first time, he felt like he could breathe again.

"Well done down there, boys," he'd said, greeting them back. "You did a great thing."

"It wasn't just us," Neil said. "It was a group effort."

"I wonder where we'll go next," Michael wondered aloud as he peered out of the window.

Armstrong stared out into the black void. It all looked a little less scary now. A little less impossible.

"The possibilities are endless."

The Apollo 11 crew splashed down in the Pacific Ocean two days later, safe inside *Columbia*. The crew were taken straight to quarantine. As nobody had ever been to the Moon before, no one knew what the risks might be, and so, to be on be safe side, the men spent three weeks locked away to make sure they were safe and healthy.

Finally they were allowed to return to the real world, and back to their old lives. But for all three of them, they knew that things would never quite be the same. Everything felt different. Earth somehow felt much smaller to them.

"Do you think you'll ever go back?" Buzz asked, looking up at the bright blue sky above them. "Neil?" He waved his hand in front of his captain's face, but Neil was lost in thought.

"Hey," laughed Buzz. "Are you on another planet or what?"

But Neil wasn't on another planet. Not yet, anyway ...

Things to think about

1. How do the astronauts feel before take-off? What words would you use to describe their feelings?
2. How do Neil and Buzz describe the Moon's surface?
3. What problems do they encounter when trying to land? Why does the mission nearly fail?
4. How do they solve the technical issues they encounter?
5. What happens when they've returned to Earth? How do they feel after the mission is over?

Write it yourself

This book retells the first Moon landing from the point of view of the astronauts who took part. Now try to write your own retelling of a different true story you know and think about the viewpoint you will tell it from.

Plan your story before you begin to write it.

Start off with a story map:

- a beginning to introduce the characters and where and when your story is set (the setting);
- a problem that the main characters will need to fix in the story;
- an ending where the problems are resolved.

Get writing! Try to include geographical and historical details so that your readers get a sense of the time and place of your story, and think about the dialogue your characters would use. Would they use formal or informal language?

Notes for parents and carers

Independent reading

The aim of independent reading is to read this book with ease. This series is designed to provide an opportunity for your child to read for pleasure and enjoyment. These notes are written for you to help your child make the most of this book.

About the book

When Neil Armstrong, Buzz Aldrin and Michael Collins set off on 16 July 1969, they booked their place in history, taking part in the first ever Moon landing. This story recreates this famous episode from the points of view of the astronauts during an incredible few days.

Before reading

Ask your child why they have selected this book. Look at the title and blurb together. What do they think it will be about? Do they think they will like it?

During reading

Encourage your child to read independently. If they get stuck on a longer word, remind them that they can find syllable chunks that can be sounded out from left to right. They can also read on in the sentence and think about what would make sense.

After reading

Support comprehension by talking about the story. What happened?
Then help your child think about the messages in the book that go beyond the story, using the questions on the page opposite. Give your child a chance to respond to the story, asking:
Did you enjoy the story and why? Who was your favourite character?
What was your favourite part? What did you expect to happen at the end?

Franklin Watts
First published in Great Britain in 2019
by The Watts Publishing Group

Copyright © The Watts Publishing Group 2019
All rights reserved.

Series Editors: Jackie Hamley, Melanie Palmer and Grace Glendinning
Series Advisors: Dr Sue Bodman and Glen Franklin
Series Designer: Peter Scoulding

A CIP catalogue record for this book is
available from the British Library.

ISBN 978 1 4451 6543 1 (hbk)
ISBN 978 1 4451 6544 8 (pbk)
ISBN 978 1 4451 7066 4 (library ebook)

Printed in China

Franklin Watts
An imprint of
Hachette Children's Group
Part of The Watts Publishing Group
Carmelite House
50 Victoria Embankment
London EC4Y 0DZ

An Hachette UK Company
www.hachette.co.uk

www.franklinwatts.co.uk

Transmission and some dialogue content adapted from NASA's
original transcript of the Apollo 11 Spacecraft Commentary

FSC
www.fsc.org
MIX
Paper from
responsible sources
FSC® C104740